Cup
Run

Martin Waddell

illustrated by Russell Ayto

WALKER BOOKS
AND SUBSIDIARIES

LONDON · BOSTON · SYDNEY

Cup Run

This is our team, the Belton Goalbusters.
The ace striker with the ball is me, Jackie D.
My mate Dipper is the one who is making
a face. The big one at the end is our other
ace striker, Farouk.

Farouk's dad filmed us in the Holt Boys' League Cup, where we had to play teams in our division, and the division above us, where there are some really good teams.

Holt Boys' League Cup
Round One

Belton Goalbusters
v
Grainger Youth Club

This is me kicking off.

This is our captain, Joe Smith, heading over the bar.

This is our goalie, Jonathan Tew, making a save.

This is Farouk shooting wide.

This is me crossing the ball, with two minutes to go.

This is Farouk out-jumping the keeper.

This is Farouk power-heading home!

This is everyone hugging Farouk.

This is the ref blowing for time.

We won 1–0, but it was a hard game because they were much bigger than us, and rough. Their defenders kept kicking Farouk and me. The ref gave them five yellow cards and we only got one.

One of their big kids said: "You're a team of whingers. You won't win the cup," as we came off the field.

"We beat you, anyway!" said Farouk.

The big kid punched Farouk. Someone told the ref. He red-carded Farouk and the kid for fighting, even though Farouk hadn't done anything.

It meant we had to play in the next round without Farouk. Farouk's dad told the ref he couldn't red-card Farouk after the whistle, but the ref didn't take any notice.

"It's not fair suspending me!" Farouk told everyone.

We all thought that we'd lose in the next round, without our star striker.

"It'll be OK," Dipper said. "We've still got Jackie D!"

It was up to me to score the goals that would get us through Round Two.

Holt Boys' League Cup
Round Two Draw

Melton Rangers v Cork Boys

East Maltby v Stream Rovers

Owen United v Metro Boys' Club

Colt Town Boys v Samsong

Billcourt Rec v Cassio Celtic

Welby United v Belton Goalbusters

Star Villa v Hillhall Rovers

Dolby Greens v West End Boys

It was a tough draw. We had to play against the team who had been our closest rivals all year in the league... But this time, without our top striker.

Holt Boys' League Cup
Round Two

Welby United
v
Belton Goalbusters

This is me scoring our first goal.

1–0 to us.

This is their equalizer. 1–1.

Whoops! This is their second goal.

I blame our keeper. 1–2.

More whoops! This is their third goal,

just before half-time. 1–3.

This is me scoring straight after kick-off
with a solo run through. 2–3.

This me scoring again with a header. 3–3.

This is Dipper scoring direct from a free kick to make it 4–3.

This is Joe Smith giving away a free kick on the edge of the box.

01:29:32

This is their free kick hitting the bar
in the last minute.

"A hat-trick for me, and we won it 4–3!
That rhymes and it makes me a poet!"
I told Farouk.

"Never mind poetry," said Farouk. "Let's
see who we get in the quarter-finals."

Holt Boys' League Cup
Quarter-final Draw

West End Boys v Melton Rangers

East Maltby v Metro Boys' Club

Colt Town Boys v Star Villa

Belton Goalbuster v Cassio Celtic

Only Goalbusters and East Maltby were still left in the cup from our division, so we knew the draw would be tough. It was, because Cassio had finished third in Division Two, with the lowest goals-against record of all four divisions.

Holt Boys' League Cup
Quarter-final

Belton Goalbusters
v
Cassio Celtic

This is their goalie saving a spot kick
from me. 0–0.

This is their goalie saving a power header
from Farouk. Still 0–0.

This is their goalie watching my header bounce off the bar. Still 0–0.

This is their brilliant breakaway goal, on the stroke of half-time. We were losing 0–1.

These diagrams show how they did it:

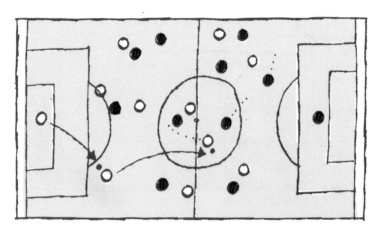

Diagram 1 Goalie to back; back to midfielder.

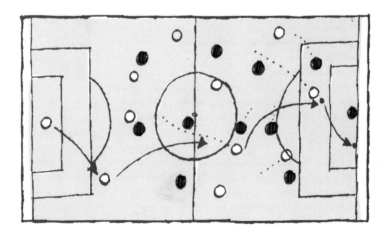

Diagram 2 Midfielder switches play
to on-running striker – GOAL!

This is their goalie tipping Dipper's free kick over the bar.

This is Farouk missing a sitter.

This is Farouk poaching our goal.

Their goalie dropped Dipper's cross. 1–1.

This is me, Jackie D, scoring our winner!
2–1.

We thought Cassio Boys were the best team that we'd played. They weren't tough like West End Boys, but they played really good stuff on the break. Their goalie was world class, too, apart from the one that he dropped, when Farouk poached his goal!

We'd made it into the semis.

Holt Boys' League Cup
Semi-final Draw

Belton Goalbusters
v
Metro Boys' Club

West End Boys
v
Star Villa

Holt Boys'
League Cup
Semi-final

Belton Goalbusters
v
Metro Boys' Club

This is their centre-back heading an own goal past his keeper. 1–0 to us.

This is Dipper scoring our second goal to make it 2–0.

This is me, Jackie D, slashing another goal home. 3–0.

This is our keeper Jonathan Tew saving a spot kick to stop their fight back! 3–0.

Then they scored. 3–1.

Then they scored again! 3–2.

This is Farouk clearing the ball off
our line.

This is Joe Smith bumping into
Jonathan Tew.

This is me clearing the ball with
Jonathan Tew flat on his back.

This is everyone cheering the whistle,
because we'd made it into the final.

Star Villa got into the final by beating West End Boys. The final was at the Rovers' ground, with a grandstand and programmes. There was a big crowd, as we were playing just before Rovers' friendly game against City.

All the Rovers fans saw us play our Cup Final!

We got a new set of jerseys sponsored by Dipper's dad's shop, so we would look good when we lifted the Cup.

Holt Boys' League Cup
Final

Star Villa
v
Belton Goalbusters

This is Rovers' ground before the crowd
turned up.

There are our supporters. Farouk's mum
is the one with the baby.

This is us in the changing-room.

This is us running out onto the pitch.

This is me winning the toss.

This is Farouk kicking off.

They almost scored in the first minute.

Then they almost did it again!

This is our goalie Jonathan Tew letting in a sitter. 0–1 to Star Villa.

This is Dipper bringing down their star striker. Penalty!

This is Jonathan tipping their spot kick over the bar for a corner. Still 0–1.

This is Jonathan missing the corner, and their striker scoring. 0–2 to Star Villa.

This is Dipper putting me clear on
the right.

This is me squaring the ball back
for Dipper.

This is Dipper trying to walk the ball
into the goal.

This is their keeper saving at Dipper's
feet. 0–2 at half-time.

This is me, Jackie D, outwitting their keeper. 1–2 to Star Villa.

This is Farouk crashing a Farouk Special into the net. 2–2.

This is Jonathan Tew breaking his wrist.

This is Farouk being brilliant in goal.

This is Dipper and me back there defending.

This is Dipper spotting my run.

This is me, Jackie D, scoring the winner! It finished 3–2 to the Belton Goalbusters!

We won the Holt Boys' League Cup the first time we were in it, playing the big teams from the division above us!

For Averil
M. W.
For Robert and Joseph
R. A.

Walker Starters

The Dragon Test by June Crebbin, illustrated by Polly Dunbar
0-7445-9018-3
Hal the Highwayman by June Crebbin, illustrated by Polly Dunbar
0-7445-9019-1
Cup Run by Martin Waddell, illustrated by Russell Ayto
0-7445-9026-4
Going Up! by Martin Waddell, illustrated by Russell Ayto
0-7445-9027-2
Big Wig by Colin West
0-7445-9017-5
Percy the Pink by Colin West
0-7445-9054-X

Series consultant: Jill Bennett, author of
Learning to Read with Picture Books

First published 2003 by
Walker Books Ltd
87 Vauxhall Walk
London SE11 5HJ

10 9 8 7 6 5 4 3 2

Text © 2003 Martin Waddell
Illustrations © 2003 Russell Ayto

The right of Martin Waddell and
Russell Ayto to be identified as
author and illustrator respectively
of this work has been asserted by
them in accordance with the
Copyright, Designs and Patents
Act 1988

This book has been typeset in
Journal Text

Printed in Hong Kong

British Library Cataloguing in Publication Data:
a catalogue record for this book is available
from the British Library

ISBN 0-7445-9026-4